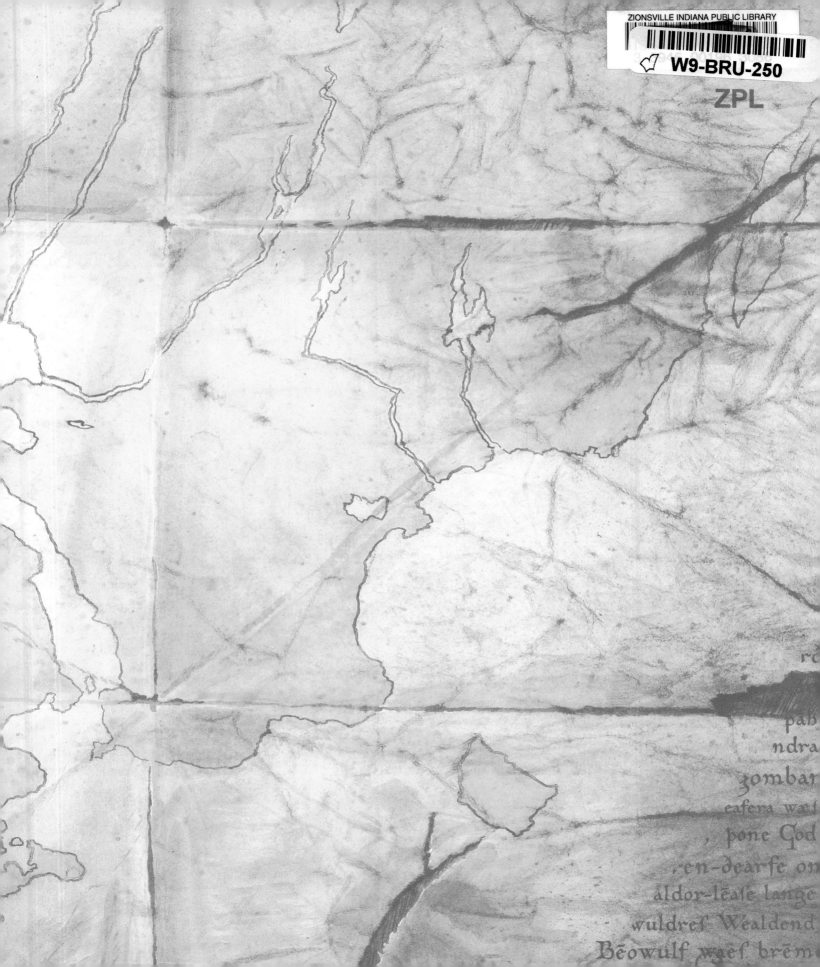

WÆT W

na in gear

m gefrun

medon.

atum,

ēah;

c

Beowulf may be a tale from the so-called Dark Ages,
but would that our own age of enlightenment
could provide flames as bright.

ƕÆT WE ᵹAR-DE

na in gear-dagum þēod-cyning
þrym gefrūnon, hū ða æþelingaſ elle
fremedon. Oft Scyld Scēfing ſceaþēn
þreatum, monegum mægþum meodo-ſetl
oftēah; egſode Eorle, ſyððan ǣreſt wear
fēaſceaft funden; hē þæſ frōfre gebā
wēox under wolcnum, weorð-myndum þā
oðþæt him ǣᵹhwylc þāra ymb-ſittendr
ofer hron-rāde hȳran ſcolde, gomba
gyldan: þæt wæſ gōd cyning! Ðǣm eafera wa
æfter cenned geong in geardum, þone ᵹo
ſende folce tō frōfre; fyren-ðearfe o
geat, þæt hīe ǣr drugon aldor-lēaſe lang
hwile; him þæſ Līf-frēa, wuldreſ Wealden
worold-āre forgeaf; Bēowulf wæſ brēm

BEOWULF

A TALE OF BLOOD, HEAT, AND ASHES

For my wife, Fataneh, and my son, Dana
J. H.

Text copyright © 2007 by Nicky Raven
Illustrations copyright © 2007 by John Howe

Selected art from this book originally appeared in
Beowulf: The Legend, by Sophisticated Games

Library of Congress Cataloging-in-Publication Data is available.
Library of Congress Catalog Card Number pending

ISBN: 978-0-7636-3647-0

2 4 6 8 10 9 7 5 3 1

Printed in China
Designed by Nghiem Ta
Edited by Ruth Martin

This book was typeset in Uncial WF and Footlight MT.
The illustrations were done in watercolor, ink, and colored pencil.

Candlewick Press
2067 Massachusetts Avenue
Cambridge, Massachusetts 02140

visit us at www.candlewick.com

CANDLEWICK PRESS
CAMBRIDGE. MASSACHUSETTS

RETOLD BY
NICKY RAVEN

BEOWULF

A TALE OF BLOOD, HEAT, AND ASHES

ILLUSTRATED BY
JOHN HOWE

BEOWULF
A TALE OF BLOOD, HEAT, AND ASHES

> hWÆT WE GAR-DE
> na in gear-dagum þēod-cyninga
> þrym gefrūnon, hū ða æþelingaſ ellen
> fremedon. Oft Scyld Scēfing ſceaþena
> þreatum, monegum mægþum meodo-ſetla
> oftēah; egſode Eorle, ſyððan ǣreſt wearð
> fēaſceaft funden; hē þæſ frōfre gebād.
> wēox under wolcnuʀ, weorð-myndum þāh.

HWÆT WE GAR-DE

na in gear-dagum þēod-cyning
þrym gefrūnon, hū ða æþelingas elle
fremedon.   Oft Scyld Scēfing sceaþen
þreatum, monegum mægþum meodo-setl
oftēah; egsode Eorle, syððan ǣrest wear
fēasceaft funden; hē þæs frōfre gebā
wēox under wolcnum, weorð-myndum þā
oðþæt him ǣghwylc þāra ymb-sittendr
ofer hron-rāde hȳran scolde, gomba
gyldan: þæt wæs gōd cyning! Ðǣm eafera wæ
æfter cenned geong in geardum, þone Go
sende folce tō frōfre;   fyren-ðearfe o
geat, þæt hīe ǣr drugon aldor-lēase lang
þwile; him þæs Līf-frēa, wuldres Wealden
worold-āre forgeaf; Bēowulf wæs brē

Beowulf

An Anglo-Saxon Poem

ð
u
ƿa
æf
veor
āra
an fc
yning!
in gear
re;   fy
rugon a
-frēa, wu
ʒeaf; Bēow

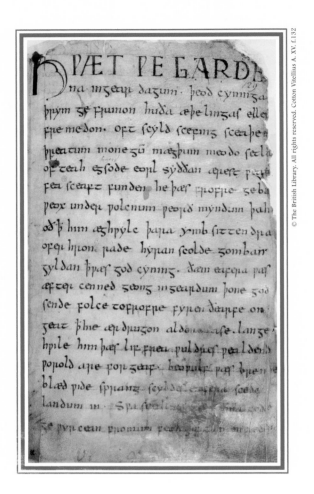

Beowulf is one of the oldest works in the English language—an Anglo-Saxon poem known only by a single manuscript dating from the early eleventh century. The original story existed perhaps 250 years earlier than the manuscript, but scholars have never agreed upon the precise date of its composition.

In 1731, that one extant manuscript was stored as part of Robert Bruce Cotton's collection in the library of Ashburnam House in Westminster, England. Here it barely survived a devastating fire that consumed hundreds of other priceless works. Today, it is stored at the British Library in London, where new technologies are being used to create a digital archive of this precious part of our literary history.

The scorched thousand-year-old manuscript describes the story of a hero—Beowulf—and his struggle against the formidable monster Grendel. Written in a rhythmic, pumping style, this poem makes the most of the natural energy and force of the Anglo-Saxon language.

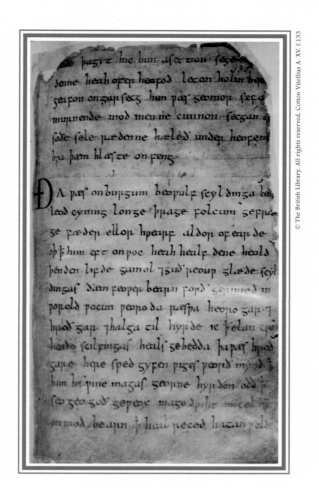

After the Romans left Britain in the fourth century AD, there were numerous invasions from the fierce warriors of northern Europe: the Vikings (from Scandinavia) and the Saxons (from Germany). This was also a time when Christians settled in northern Europe, bringing with them tales of new heroes. Beowulf is one such early Christian hero—one of a tribe known as the Geats, who once occupied part of southern Sweden. From these historical beginnings, the ancient tale of *Beowulf* emerged and has been passed down through the ages.

The inspiring influence of this great work continues today, supported by more modern translations such as that of William Morris, designer and poet, in 1895, and the celebrated version by Seamus Heaney in 1999. Here, in this retelling of the epic adventure, we focus on the most exciting parts of Beowulf's tale. We go back to a harsh time, where dangers lurked at every turn. You are about to enter a world of tough men and merciless monsters, for this is a tale of blood, heat, and ashes.

wonsceaft wera. Wiht unhælo,
grim ond grædig, gearo sóna wæs,
réoc ond réþe, ond on ræste genam
þrítig þegna; þanon eft gewat
húðe hrémig tó hám faran
mid þære wæl-fylle wíca néosan
Ða wæs on úhtan mid ær-dæge
Grendles gúð-cræft gumum undyrne
þá wæs æfter wiste wóp up áhafen
micel morgen-swég. Mære þéoden
æþeling ær-góð, unblíðe sæt
þolode ðrýð-swýð, þegn-sorge dréah
syðþan híe þæs laðen lást scéawedon
wergen gáste. Wæs þæt gewin tó strang
láð ond longsum. Næs hit lengra fyrst
ac ymb áne niht eft gefremed
morð-beala máre ond nó mearn fore
fæhðe ond fyrene; wæs tó fæst on þám

The Story Begins....

veor

āra

an ſc

yning!

ın gear

re; fy

rugon a

-frēa, wul

ȝeaf; Bēow

wonsceaft wera. Wiht unhælo,
grim ond grædig, gearo sōna wæs
rēoc ond rēþe, ond on ræste genām
þrītig þegna; þanon eft gewat
hūðe hrēmig tō hām faran
mid þære wæl-fylle wīca nēosan
Ða wæs on ūhtan mid ær-dæge
Grendles gūð-cræft gumum undyrne
þā wæs æfter wiste wōp up āhafen
micel morgen-swēg. Mære þēoden
æþeling ær-gōd, unblīðe sæt
þolode ðrȳð-swȳð, þegn-sorge drēah
syðþan hīe þæs laðen lāst scēawedon
wergen gāste. Wæs þæt gewin tō strang
lāð ond longsum. Næs hit lengra fyrst
ac ymb āne niht eft gefremede
morð-beala māre ond nō mearn fore
fæhðe ond fyrene; wæs tō fæst on þā

IT HAD LIVED IN THIS STINKING PLACE FOR GENERATIONS OF MEN.

Defeated and driven into hiding by heroes of other days, it had sought out this damp, dark, miserable place in which to fester and dream of revenge. It was a thing of nightmares, a creature of tales told to make children behave. A fearful, furtive thing, it lived in the damp lands, feeding on fish, frogs, and unsuspecting birds that came there thinking to be predator, not prey. But throughout these years it had dreamed of a different meal— occasionally a scent wafted across the mire, fueling those fantasies. And now the scent was stronger, closer. The urges were more powerful, the hunger grew, and the beast moaned in its sleep as its need for meat fought the fear in its cowardly heart.

CHAPTER ONE
HROTHGAR'S HALL

I had heard tales of Heorot, the hall of mighty Lord Hrothgar, but the sight of it exceeded all my imaginings. Ours was a wintry and violent land; dwellings were built for defense against the elements and against raiders. Not that such defenses prevented our home from being burned to the ground or spared us the slaughter of our family. That's why we came here, my brother and I—we needed a home, and great lords always need fighters. I am Wiglaf. Then I was nobody, a boy from the Dane lands, full of sorrow and eager to fight.

The hall was built at the top of a mound, with a half mile of cleared land around it. Beyond that it was protected on three sides by the forest and on the fourth by the great river. Beyond the river was the mire, a bleak, soulless place with a bad reputation. It would take a brave band of raiders to attack through the mire.

Whether it was the dark and the damp, or thoughts of my lost family surfacing, the first sight of that great building sent an involuntary shudder down my spine, and I felt a trickle of sweat under my leathers and furs, despite the cold. I looked at my brother—he must have sensed my unease, for he smiled and clasped my shoulder.

"How do you like your new home, Wiglaf?" he jested, and I was surprised to hear an edge of uncertainty in his voice. Even Preben, who had once wrestled and killed a wolf with

I took a closer look at the massive timbered building in front of me. Even in the half-light of the torches it was magnificent. Two huge beams the width of three men and the height of six rose on either side of the doorway, supporting a network of other massive planks and beams. Runes and carvings were cut into every available flat surface, for the carpenters and builders liked to leave reminders of their art. The doorway itself was built for defense. No more than two men could stand side by side in it, but even the briefest glance told of the thickness and durability of the ancient wood. A golden carving of a serpent—the sign of Hrothgar's house—was planted firmly in the center; the creature's jeweled eye seemed to bore into the heart of any who approached.

Those first few months at Heorot were heady days and gave no hint of the bleak times that lay ahead. We hunted, we fought, we drank, we sang, we slept. The harvests were good, the hall was never short of ale, and the pretty girls were always ready with a kiss for a brave young fighter. But then came the troubles. They started the night of a grand feast thrown in honor of a troop of warriors, myself and Preben included, who had wiped out a marauding nest of bandits. The drinking and singing had gone on into the early hours, until most of the men had simply fallen asleep where they sat. The rest of us lay curled up on benches and furs at the edges of the hall, barely awake and blissfully unaware of the danger that lurked beyond the walls.

Outside, the dark thing stumbled through the night, the oozy wetness of the marshes slapping and sucking at its scaly limbs. The beast panted and slavered, half in anticipation of the bloody feast it dreamed of, half in dread of the steel that it feared was waiting. But it could not turn back. Driven to madness and despair by the smells of food, smoke, and ale borne on the wind, and tormented by the snatches of laughter and song that mocked its wretched existence, the monster lurched toward Heorot.

Preben was in the group to take first watch and joined some others huddled around a small fire in the narrow entry passage that served as a lobby to the main hall. It was this group that bore the brunt of the beast's attack.

I remember being awoken by the enormous crash as the beast beat open the front gates of Heorot. Hazy as I was with ale and lack of sleep, it took a few moments before the ruckus penetrated my consciousness. We were under attack! Throwing on my jerkin and hastily thrusting my feet into my boots, I seized my ax and shield and joined the other warriors stumbling haphazardly toward the source of the trouble.

I had seen many fights in the previous months, some of them savage and bloody with no quarter on either side, but never had I witnessed slaughter like this. A nightmarish vision stood in the inner lobby. Stooping to fit inside, the creature loomed twice the height of the burly men hacking at it with their blades. The long, jointed limbs that swung relentlessly made it hard to reach the beast to strike. As I watched, one warrior ducked under a swinging arm to drive his sword into the monster's side, only for the iron blade to slide harmlessly off the dark, scaly hide. Before he could retreat, the other monstrous arm seized the warrior by the shoulder and lifted him clean off the ground. The beast's powerful jaws opened to reveal an obscene cave of a mouth, lined with teeth like rows of daggers, dripping with blood and strings of flesh.

By now there were forty or fifty warriors crowding to the attack. Moving with unnatural speed, the beast darted to the left and seized two figures cowering by the wall; spinning around, it dashed for the hallway, slashing its way through the remaining warriors into the dark of the night. No one gave chase; no one even spoke for many minutes. The carnage was sickening. Torn bodies and limbs lay on the hallway floor like cuts of meat in a slaughterhouse. The smell of blood and fear and death filled the nostrils and emptied the soul.

The creature lurched across the open ground, looking behind for
a sign of the iron-men giving chase, but none came. It slowed to a
more regular lurching gait. The warriors under its arm were still
howling and wailing. It didn't like the noise; so it crunched them
with its jaws to stop the wailing. The noise stopped.

Its appetite whetted, the beast came again the next night. This
time we were prepared, armed and tense, not relaxed and stupefied
with drink, but the outcome was little different. Our weapons made
no impression on the beast's hide, and its strength, speed, and reach
meant that any who tried to get close enough to grapple were
shredded by its fierce claws.

Over the next month, I saw many good fighters and good friends
fall prey to this ravenous creature. Wise men were consulted;
we asked if they knew any way to bring down this fearsome
opponent. They told us the monster was named Grendel and had
existed for generations of Man, beyond our time and knowledge.

At the end of the month I was summoned by Lord Hrothgar.
"Wiglaf," he said quietly, his fingers drumming nervously on the
arm of his great chair. "My hall is almost emptied of warriors; no
one dares sleep here, and the good times and the singing have ceased.
We can no longer fight this monster alone. You must travel to the
land of the Geats across the sea and ask aid of Hygelac, their king.
I have heard of a mighty warrior who dwells among them. He may
be our last chance."

CHAPTER TWO
SEARCH FOR THE HERO

I was no seafarer; I had been chosen for the journey due
to my tact and courtesy. The sailing was not long or rough,
but it took me days to find my sea legs, and the experienced
warriors laughed and teased me, saying that I should wear
a skirt and work in the galley. After little more than a week,
and much to my relief, we arrived. There wasa watch on the
coast, archers and horsemen, so we splashed through the
shallows with our spears and shields reversed as a sign of peace.
The urgency of our need was clear to the captain of the watch—
three of my companions and I were given swift horses and
leave to travel inland to the Hall of Hygelac.

Hygelac, King of the Geats, was older than I expected—
older than most in the harsh northern lands. His shoulders were
stooped and his beard white as snow, but a fire still shone in
his keen eyes, and he spoke clearly.

"Welcome, young Dane, to my hall. You have news from
Hrothgar?" he asked.

"I do, Lord Hygelac, but only bad news," I replied. "Our land
is ravaged by a monster from the coastal marshes. Grendel, this
Night Stalker, brings fear and death to Hrothgar's hall, Heorot,
and is a plague on all the land around. If Grendel is allowed to
continue, then the House of Hrothgar will fall, and the land
of the Danes will return to the old, lawless ways."

"You bring grave news indeed," mused the king. "But how
can I help? If the best fighting men of mighty Hrothgar cannot
prevail, then what can we do?"

I thought for a moment and looked around the hall. Hygelac was surrounded by his chief thanes and warriors. All were stern, seasoned men, but there was one, a young man, who caught my gaze. Blond-haired and gray-eyed like the rest, but with half a head more height and massive girth in the shoulders, he looked every inch a champion. The warrior caught my glance, gave a small smile, and took a pace forward.

"I believe I know what is on this young man's mind," said the warrior. "I believe it is I whom he seeks. Did Hrothgar not instruct you to seek out a champion among the Geats?"

It was barely a question, and I simply nodded by way of reply.

The king stood. "I cannot permit this, Beowulf. I am sorry indeed for the problems of Hrothgar, for he has been a good ally to us in the past, but I cannot spare my best champion in the cause of another land."

"But you know my history, my lord king," said the warrior Beowulf, inclining his head respectfully toward his master. "There is blood-debt to be paid here. My honor says I must go. And having brought peace to this land, I long to feel the salt of the sea wind on my lips again and smell once more the air of the land of my birth."

The king's shoulders slumped at these words, and some of the sparkle in his eyes seemed to disappear.

"You're right," he agreed, barely audible. "I cannot speak against the blood."

I was intrigued by this exchange and eager to know more of this warrior. I had not long to wait.

So quickly was the matter agreed that we were at sea again within three days. The return journey was made in haste with favorable winds and extra shoulders at the oars. Beowulf brought with him a band of his closest companions, among them his kinsman Waegmund, Scaife the One-Eye, and Handscio, a young warrior whom Beowulf had rescued in an earlier adventure and who now followed him like a faithful hound.

Aboard ship, Beowulf told me his history with the Danes. His father, Edgetheow, a Geat who had fallen foul of the law, had taken refuge with Hrothgar, who was then but a young lordling under threat and short of allies. He had become Hrothgar's right-hand man, fighting alongside him as he sought to bring the rule of law and stability to the southern Danes. Edgetheow had with him his young wife, and she bore him a son, whom they called Beowulf. While Beowulf was still a young boy of six, a message from the Court of the Geats reached Edgetheow; he was summoned back to serve Hygelac and given a full pardon. Before he left Hrothgar's hall, Edgetheow swore an oath that should ever the Danish king be in need, he, and in turn his kin, would come immediately to the Dane's aid.

As I listened to Beowulf talk and learned more of the man, I was filled with hope; here was an exceptional man, a natural leader, a true warrior. If any man could put an end to the devastation of the Night Stalker, it was this Beowulf. Such newfound optimism evaporated within an hour of landing back in Danish lands. The coast warden greeted us formally and courteously, but his eyes would not meet mine and I knew something was amiss. As we neared Heorot, I called out to several of my battle companions whom we saw along the way; they acknowledged my greeting, but they too looked away hastily. Tales tell of a sense of foreboding—I knew now what they meant. Something was wrong, and deep down I knew what it was. My brother had always been one of the first into the fray; he was tough and fearless and seemed to believe in his own invincibility. But now I knew that he was no more invincible than any of the others slain by this foul beast.

At last we stood, the fifteen Geats and I, in front of Hrothgar.
"Wiglaf," he began gravely.
"I know, Lord Hrothgar," I replied before he could continue. "I sensed it the moment we arrived. The monster?"
Hrothgar nodded. "Aye, the monster. But even in death it may be that your brother showed us the way to defeat it. As the monster swung

its arms, Preben got inside its reach and flung himself around
the creature's legs, trying to bring them to the ground.
If another could have reached him to lend power to his efforts,
then we might have toppled this Grendel."

I blinked back my stinging tears and stepped aside to usher
forth the champion of the Geats.

"My Lord Hrothgar, this is Beowulf of the Geats. You will
remember him only as a small boy in your hall, but here he is,
a man now, and come to our aid in fulfillment of his father's oath."

At this Hrothgar's back straightened, and he leaned forward
in his chair with interest.

"It is I, Lord Hrothgar, come to honor my father's blood-debt,"
began Beowulf.

"You were a strapping boy even at six—but look at you now!"
said the king, and for a moment a ghost of a smile flickered
across his grief-strewn face.

"Indeed," replied Beowulf courteously. "Maybe it is the good
Danish air I breathed as a boy that helped me reach this stature."

Hrothgar laughed and stood up. He stepped down from his
great chair and clasped Beowulf in his arms.

"You are most welcome to Heorot, Beowulf; I only wish it
were in better times."

Beowulf knelt and kissed the old lord's hand. "I am here to
bring back the better times. I shall bring you the head of this
creature and return to my own land in triumph, or I shall not
return at all."

It was agreed that the Geats would rest that night and take
up their vigil against the coming of Grendel the following
evening. I walked the length of Hrothgar's estate the next day,
persuading all I could to join me in sharing the watch with
the newcomers. It was a near-thankless task; the Danes were
sick of the bloodshed and mayhem, and most were ready to
quit and seek shelter and employment elsewhere. I was ashamed
when I reported to Beowulf that night with no more than
a dozen men, most of them close friends of Preben.

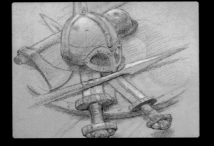

That first night of our watch, all was quiet, and the second and third nights were the same. Beowulf made use of the time, lost in thought, his head resting on his arms as he lay on the long benches in Hrothgar's hall. On the fourth day he called for long, sharpened wooden staves, such as might be found protecting a palisade. Puzzled, we gathered around as our new leader outlined his plan; some objected, but there was something about Beowulf's manner that quieted even the most vociferous of the Danes.

Our chance to put the plan into action came that night. In the dim hours we heard the now-familiar snorting around the portal to the hall. Drunk on its previous conquests, the beast threw its weight against the door—there was no need, for this time it was unbolted. Lurching into the hall, Grendel let forth a bellow of rage as it saw the warriors ranged before it and leaped toward the nearest with unnatural agility. The bellow turned to a furious and concentrated roar as the creature's assault met not with an ineffectual blade and the satisfying crunch of bone between its teeth but with the iron-banded end of half a dozen staves wielded by hardened men who refused to quail before the Night Stalker's grisly presence. The beast turned and launched itself at the group of Danes I was leading, but again met with a barricade of sharpened wood. The creature swung its long, clawed limbs in vain, and its furious howls grew shriller and angrier.

The battle seemed like an eternity of darkness and tension, but we kept our discipline and eventually Grendel tired.

The monster's swinging arms moved in a less deadly arc, and the slavering jaws were too weary to spew forth much venom and rage. The beast knew that it would get no kill tonight and turned to make its retreat. Beowulf seized his moment. As Grendel's back turned, he leaped atop the monster's shoulders and flung his arms around the enormous neck. Even with his great reach, the Geat could barely stretch around the beast's colossal frame. With a mighty bellow and a surge of new energy, the monster threw back its shoulders and almost sent the Geat spinning from his perch. Beowulf kept his balance, though he was sliding from the beast's shoulders. As he slid, he managed to loop an arm around Grendel's shoulder and cling on, but even as he locked the monster's left arm, he was in grave danger from the swinging right. Grendel swung twice with its free limb, one swing a hairbreadth from decapitating Beowulf, and the other striking a glancing blow that rattled the Geat's armored helm. As the arm swung back for a third, deadly blow, a figure detached itself from the phalanx of stave-wielding warriors. Handscio seized the flailing arm and clung on. Pinned to the spot by the battling warriors, Grendel had just one remaining course of action. With a mighty heave, the Night Stalker pulled Handscio toward its brutal cavern of a mouth— the young Geat stood no chance; no armor in the world could withstand those fangs. Handscio's last act was to ram his stave into Grendel's baleful eye moments before the monster closed its jaws and the warrior's blood spattered across the walls.

The beast's howls as it registered its pain were piercing, but even they were drowned by Beowulf's deafening roar of fury as he saw the demise of his friend. Fired by anger and grief, the powerful warrior braced his feet against the mighty door frame and pulled on the monster's shoulder with every last fragment of strength in his battle-weary muscles. Enraged and partly blinded, the monster recoiled and threw itself in the opposite direction. There was a gargantuan crack as bone and flesh parted and stentorian howls of anguish issued from the beast. Grendel leaped out of the doorway before any of us could follow, and Beowulf, with all his weight propelling him the other way, was flung head over heels onto a bench, where he lay, momentarily stunned. In his hands, still twitching in a ghastly, ghostly way, was Grendel's arm—scaly, sinewy, and severed.

There was a momentary hush in the hall, part exhaustion, part disbelief. Then, with a mighty shout, the warriors surged forward to acclaim their leader.

Beowulf struggled to his feet, still bewildered. He pushed away his admirers and walked to the broken body of Handscio, his young follower. He cradled the youngster's ruined and blood-drenched remains and closed the dead, staring, pain-filled eyes. This simple display of respect and affection quieted the onlookers, who were growing rapidly in number as news of the triumph spread throughout the holding. But soon the tongues were wagging again, and the questioning resumed. By the time Hrothgar arrived at the hall to greet the exhausted warriors, a huge throng had gathered and wildly exaggerated tales of the fight were spreading.

Hrothgar sat on his great chair with his counselor, Ashhere, by his side. The sea of folk in front of him swayed noisily back and forth, but he waited patiently. The mass parted at last to make way for a small knot of warriors, Danes and Geats both. This knot parted, too, to reveal one man carrying a grisly trophy in both his arms.

"Lord Hrothgar," said the warrior, "I have failed you."

Hrothgar appeared to mull over these words carefully for a while before replying.

"In what way have you failed, Beowulf?"

"I promised you the head of this creature that has plagued your hall," replied the Geat, masking a grin as he feigned deep sadness. "But see, I bring only an arm."

"I think for now, Beowulf," Hrothgar said, "we shall let him keep his head. For you have rendered him armless!"

The warrior and the lord continued to look at each other, the corners of their mouths twitching. Hrothgar threw back his head and roared with laughter. He leaped from his seat and flung his arms around the exhausted Geat.

"Drinks, here, drinks for the hero, the monster-slayer!" he shouted to his entourage, "and hang our trophy for all to see." A huge cheer rang around the room, and the hubbub swelled again around the party in the center. It soon grew hot, and I still had the stench of blood in my nose, so I made my way to the great door. Dawn was breaking, bringing a magical glitter to the frost rime on the hard ground. The early light picked out a trail of black-blue slime where the retreating monster's blood had pumped from its gaping wound. Not for a long time had the morning sun felt so good.

The pain was something the monster had never felt before. It had known misery and hunger and loneliness, but never this white-hot intense shock of ill-being. As it lurched away from the iron-men's hall with its long strides, it heard an unfamiliar sound. It was its own breath coming in ragged gasps as its life-blood ebbed from the cavernous wound in its shoulder. Somehow it kept going, staggering through the mire and plunging into the stagnant waters above its home. Drifting rather than swimming, it was unaware of how it got from the water to the floor of the murky cavern. The creature's eyes opened, glazed and unfocused. Another pair of eyes, watery and large and white, stared back. The beast's last thought as it slipped into unconsciousness and death was of its mother.

The celebration that followed that night was one of the grandest Hrothgar's hall had seen. The cooks labored from dawn till dusk under Ashhere's supervision, and the singers and tale-tellers and other entertainers were summoned. Extra ale was begged from smaller villages and halls nearby, and two of the finest prize pigs were chosen to be roasted for the centerpiece of the feast in Beowulf's honor. Grendel's torn stump was sewn up and nailed above Hrothgar's seat for all to see—the cooks' helpers spent almost as much time chasing wide-eyed children away from this freakish sight as they did stirring and chopping and fetching and carrying.

The feast began not long after dark. The Danes were seated and I was sent to fetch the Geats from their quarters. As Beowulf entered the room, all eyes turned to him. He walked forward down the ranks of seated warriors, and as he passed each table, those warriors stood, clashed their beer mugs loudly on the table, and stamped their feet in approval. By the time he reached Hrothgar's chair, the clamor was deafening. The tankards slammed in time as the Geat's name echoed over and over again in a rhythmic chant. When Beowulf reached the top of the hall, even Lord Hrothgar stood. Smiling, the chieftain, most powerful in the Danish lands, held his hands aloft for silence. It came—eventually. Hrothgar stepped to the side of his great carved chair. He gestured to his ally to sit.

"Tonight, my friend," said Hrothgar, "the hall is yours."

Beowulf looked embarrassed, but he could hardly refuse such an honor. He nodded to Hrothgar and took his place in the great carved seat. The feast was long and noisy and hot, and it was a relief when all the food was gone and we were able to push back chairs and enjoy the entertainment. The songsmiths and lore-masters tried hard to outdo each other with absurd and inaccurate versions of the fight. As the last one quieted, a sharp voice piped up from Beowulf's left.

"Which of these gaudy tales pleased you the most, friend Beowulf?" asked the voice. I looked at the speaker and frowned, for it was Unferth. Once Hrothgar's favorite, a fondness for ale had reduced Unferth's worth and made him bitter and twisted. There was now an undercurrent to his words.

"Be careful how you reply, Beowulf," I cautioned the Geat. "This Unferth thinks himself a wit and likes to bandy words."

Unferth fixed his weaselly eyes on me. "I would beware if I were you, young Wiglaf," he sneered. "Beowulf has a bad record for keeping his adoring young followers alive."

One or two of the Geats sprang to their feet at these sour words, ready to remonstrate with Unferth, but Beowulf motioned them to sit. He took a slow drink and fixed his eyes piercingly on the spiteful Dane.

"Your point is, Unferth?"

"My point is that it seems you are happy to take all the credit for this triumph, when in fact it is your dead sword-mate who should be receiving the accolades. It seems the great Beowulf is happy to let his friends die for him and enjoy the applause." Beowulf looked calmly at Unferth, but I could see he was struggling to retain his poise. Someone had to deflate the tension of the situation.

"My lord Hrothgar," I started, "I beg your permission to add one more story to the evening's entertainment. Unferth is right that young Handscio should be given honor at this table, so I would honor him by telling how he came to be at Beowulf's side—a tale I heard from his own lips on the sea-crossing." Hrothgar was wise and saw my plan immediately, nodding his assent.

Handscio was a good young man, keen to learn and eager to please. He was turning into a fine warrior—he could even write and read a little, setting him apart from the others. One day his camp was raided, but Handscio was one of the fortunate ones. Knocked unconscious by a lucky blow, he lay stunned throughout the brief fight as the raiders ransacked and looted his grandfather's holding. His family was beaten and killed, and almost all Handscio's friends died in the fight. Handscio and two others were trussed and bound to be sold as slaves by these raiders. The scum were still celebrating "a good day's work" when a hunting party fell upon them. With only three companions, the leader of the newcomers led an assault on the heavily armed campsite and the vile bandits.

The cowardly looters fell before the heroes like wheat before a scythe, for this was Beowulf the Geat, and at his back was Scaife the One-Eye, his two swords flickering like tongues of crackling steel flame. The raiders would kill their prisoners rather than lose them, and Handscio's two companions were slain where they lay, bound and gagged. As the sword rose for a third stroke, the fighter wielding it paused, and a look of amazement crossed his face. No hand held the huge ax that stuck from his chest, for it had been thrown a full twenty yards to sink itself into its target. The raider sank to his knees and made a low gurgling sound. Blood spewed from his lips, and he toppled slowly sideways, dead. Moments later Handscio felt his bonds loosened, and a voice said, "Follow, boy. Stay close."

Seizing the dead raider's sword, Handscio did as he was told. The odds still looked grim. One of the Geats was down, and the three remaining — plus Handscio — were surrounded by twenty or more fighters. Beowulf shrugged off his shield and hefted his great war-ax in both hands. Handscio glanced at him — Beowulf had a strange but calm look about him, a look that held no recognition of danger or fear, and no inclination of the concepts of defeat and death. Scaife the One-Eye had a wilder look, his mouth pulled back in what could have been a snarl but could just as easily have been a grin. The two looked at each other, nodded, and charged. The fight lasted moments: the moments it took for the two heroes to cut down half a dozen of their opponents, the moments it took for the rest to realize that this was certain death staring them in the face and take to their cowardly heels.

This was how Handscio was rescued by Beowulf. Little wonder the youngster was all too happy to lay down his life to help his friend and mentor.

I ended with a glare at Unferth, challenging him to mock, but he merely scowled into his beer and sat back. I caught Beowulf's eye, and he acknowledged me with an almost imperceptible nod of the head.

With the good mood restored, the drinking and carousing continued. Hrothgar announced that there would be gifts for the Geats, and helmets and weapons were brought forth from the armory in payment for their courage. Beowulf tried to wave away the gifts, but Hrothgar was insistent.

"This is a small price to pay for keeping my kingdom, my friend," he assured the Geat with a smile. "And tomorrow you shall have the finest gift I can bestow—a horse from my own private stables."

With these words he clapped his hands, and the queen and the ladies of the court came forth with more gifts for the Geats. Jewels and finely sewn tunics were brought out, wrapped and scented by the queen's own hand.

"Gifts for your women at home," she explained, "for by sparing their brothers and sons and husbands, they too have sacrificed for the Danes."

The Danes roared their drunken approval of their queen, and she bowed out of the hall with her ladies, leaving the talk to return to fighting and drinking and recent conquests.

The next visitor was another female, but she announced herself very differently. The door was smashed in and the bodies of the night's sentries were flung past the wreckage to lie broken and bloody on the hall floor. Then Grendel's mother strode through the opening, howling and spoiling for blood. She swung her arms at the nearest tables, smashing men, tankards, and food platters to the ground. All eyes were facing front now, as the Danes took in the full view of the latest nightmare in their hall, who was baying her grief and her thirst for revenge.

Scaled and armored like her son, Grendel's mother was a full head taller, if slimmer. Her limbs, too, were sleeker, and her chest had some semblance of femininity. There was no mistaking who she was. Her face was leaner, and her yawning mouth was not as wide as her son's—but the teeth were like two rows of sharpened daggers.

As if to demonstrate their keenness, she seized Ashhe
Hrothgar's counselor, who was standing near the door,
his head clean from his body. She spat the unfortunate
head out and greedily drank the blood from the headle
The beast tossed the body aside and seized two more h
victims. Dashing their brains out against the wall, she
off into the night, one under each arm, bellowing her

Hrothgar sat with his head in his hands, rocking ba
forth, unable to believe that the ravages had begun all
again and stricken with grief for his dear old friend. Ev
was shouting—fear and panic had gripped the room. C
alone was calm amid the storm. Beowulf sat, impassiv
his chair. He looked at Scaife and raised an eyebrow. S
grimaced and nodded in unspoken consent, then slippe
from his seat and out of the room.

his great hands.

"I had begun to suspect as much, Lord Hrothgar. Your wise men are fools," he said firmly. "They should have guessed. However inhuman and vile a monster, it must have had a mother. And however inhuman and vile the mother, a dam will always feel love for that which she nursed."

"But what are we to do, Beowulf?" asked Hrothgar faintly, almost pleading with the Geat.

"We kill her," answered Beowulf. "Even now, Scaife tracks the beast to her lair. She feeds at night, so we shall find her in daylight, when she is weakest. Grendel's mother dies tomorrow."

CHAPTER FOUR
INTO THE DEPTHS

The following dawn was very different from the one that had just passed. As if to reflect the changing mood, the sky barely lightened, and baleful clouds hung low over the land. Cold, soaking rain fell in wind-driven gusts, and the ground was damp and sodden and slippery. It was a grim party that set out behind Scaife toward the mire. The fourteen remaining Geats were joined by the same group of Danish warriors who had helped with the defense against Grendel, with one addition. To my amazement, as we were ready to leave, another horse appeared around the corner of the hall. Astride it, a trifle the worse for the drink, but looking warrior-like and grim nonetheless, was Unferth, a round shield strapped to his chest and a huge sword strapped to his back.

"No fuss, boy," he growled at me as he passed to join the column of horsemen. "It's too crabby and foul a morning for banter and wordplay."

Beowulf, at the head of the riders, swung his horse around to identify the newcomer. He saw Unferth, nodded, and smiled his distinctive smile-that-wasn't-a-smile. That done, he wheeled around once more, and the column set off. It took scarcely any time to reach the fringes of the mire, but crossing that foul place was slow going on horseback. The horses would lose their footing and slip into stagnant, sticky pools. Odd sounds would reach us out of the mist and startle our mounts—croakings and hissings and noises suggestive of creatures better left unseen. The trees and shrubs in that place were odd, contorted and stunted, and all covered with a brackish slime. Even in the cold, the mire made us sweat under our cloaks, and the cloying smell of damp vegetation coated the nostrils and made our heads ache.

It was a relief when the damp lands gave way to the dunes that heralded the coastline. It had taken only half a day to reach this place, but the horses looked as though they had traveled for twice as long and even the most seasoned warriors among us were glad to be clear of the mire. The dunes were sandy, mixed with rocks and tufts of hardy grass, and the footing was still difficult for the horses, but they moved with a spring in their step now, sensing journey's end in the tangy sea air.

We halted at a signal from Scaife, and the horses were tethered on the stubby grass. One-Eye led us across the last stretch of dunes to a small point where the stream that ran through the mere created a waterfall. Beowulf looked at Scaife. Scaife shrugged and pointed to the churning waters in the large pool below the fall.

"In there?" asked Beowulf incredulously.

"Yes," confirmed Scaife, "but let me show you something else."

Ropes were tied to two of the strongest horses. Beowulf and Scaife lowered themselves over the cliff's edge and dropped some forty feet below the top. When they reappeared, Beowulf shook his head and smiled at his friend, clapping him on the back.

"Scaife has seen a cave," he called to the rest of us, "way down below, just above the waterline. You can't see it from here, but it is there."

"So how did Scaife see it?" I asked, raising an eyebrow at the enigmatic warrior.

"Because I looked for it," One-Eye answered for himself. "The beast was heading home; that much was clear. She plunged off the cliff into the water—and I could not conceive of any reason why she would kill herself, so I assumed she was continuing her journey home. Nothing about her physiognomy suggested that she could breathe underwater, so I guessed there must be a dwelling place of sorts above the level of the pool below."

One of the warriors gave a low whistle to show he was impressed. I nodded in agreement.

"Brains to go with bravery, Scaife," I said, smiling at One-Eye. "A dangerous combination."

Scaife shrugged again. Beowulf laughed at his phlegmatic friend, and then his expression turned serious. "My friends, I thank you for accompanying me, but from here I must go on alone."

As the warriors, both Danish and Geat, began to protest, Scaife interrupted.

"How long can any one of you hold his breath underwater?" he barked. "The cave is a long way below the higher level of the pool. To climb down would be impossible. The only way to reach the cave is to swim down. The only man with lungs big enough to make the swim is Beowulf. He must go alone."

There was silence. None would admit it, but mixed in with the guilt of having to leave the onus of battle with our leader once again was a sense of relief that we didn't have to undertake what could be a suicidal mission.

The ropes were hauled up and repositioned close to the head of the fall. Beowulf prepared to enter the water. Scaife handed him a cloth soaked in oil to coat his arms and legs—it would protect him against the cold water. Beowulf looked at the weapons strapped to his horse. He turned, frowning.

"Is there any benefit in taking a weapon?" he asked aloud, though the question was for himself.

"There may be in this one," replied a voice. Unferth had unstrapped the huge blade across his back and offered it to Beowulf. "This was given to me many years ago by a wise man I met on my travels, far to the south of here."

"A generous gift, Unferth," replied Beowulf, "but I could never swim carrying this, and no sword can harm these creatures."

"This was no ordinary wise man, Lord Beowulf," said Unferth with a knowing smile, "and this is no ordinary blade." He drew the blade from its scabbard, and there was a murmur of approval from the onlooking warriors. Instead of the dull metal of most blades, this had a sheen to it, like a polished gemstone. The murmurs turned to cries of astonishment when Unferth flipped the sword in the air as if it were a child's toy and caught it after it turned a lazy, graceful circle in the air. He offered it again to Beowulf, who reached for it, eyes wide with excitement. He held the sword up and looked along its length.

"Perfect," he said. He paused and looked at Unferth, a notion of suspicion in his glance.

"Why, Unferth?" he asked, puzzled at the old warrior's change of heart.

"There was once a warrior like you," replied Unferth cryptically. "He was considered one of the finest warriors in the Dane lands, head and shoulders above other fighters. Everyone praised him and roared their approval of his deeds until he grew vain and proud. His vanity made him lazy, and he lived on tales of his deeds rather than new deeds, and he began to hate himself and call himself a coward. He became bitter and a shadow of the man he once was. An old man now, when he sees young warriors at the height of their power, he feels shame and guilt and says harsh things to mask his feelings. He would have you know that you are the finest he has seen."

Beowulf didn't reply. Instead he took a pace forward and grasped the older man in a fierce clasp. He drew back and looked Unferth in the eye. "The weak ones sit at home waiting for news, Unferth," he told him. "Only the boldest and most courageous followed me here."

Soon Beowulf stood at the edge of the cliff, his watery destiny below him. Without a backward glance, he grasped the rope and lowered himself over. The rope fell short of the pool by a few feet, and Beowulf had to drop into the freezing waters. He didn't hesitate; we saw the last heave of his shoulders as he drew a deep breath into those gargantuan lungs, and then he fell.

She saw him enter the water, her eyes accustomed to the murky blue-black depths. His movements were strong and purposeful, betraying none of the fear these creatures usually showed. She knew in her heart that this was her son's killer, and she thirsted for revenge. The sea serpents with which she shared the scraps of her kills moved to intercept the warrior, but she knew they would be no match for his courage and his keen blade. He battled his way through the monsters; she could see his face now, strong and proud, even with the strain of holding his breath. The blood of the serpents added a purplish ichor to the waters, and she lost sight of the warrior momentarily.

The hag peered into the gloom, searching for a sign of the warrior's approach, not daring to hope that he might have fallen to the serpents. She sensed rather than saw the movement to her left as he hauled himself from the water into the cave. He was cunning as well as strong and brave. There was silence as the warrior rested patiently, drawing the air back into his burning lungs. She crouched lower, feigning sleep as he approached from the far side of the cave opening. She heard him take a few paces back to avoid being seen and heard the hiss of his breath as the dim sunlight caught the interior of the cave. The bones and carcasses of her kills decked the floor; the hag grinned fiercely to herself as she realized the warrior must have recoiled at the sight of the bloody remnants of his friends.

She heard him exhale again, softly, composing himself, and then again came the soft tread of cautious feet on the stone floor. He was close now, and he paused. She knew he must be unsheathing his blade, and felt for her own, concealed in her lap. She felt the breath of air as the warrior rushed the last few steps, heard the sweep of the sword, and exulted at the grunt of surprise as her weapon came up, swift as a darting fish, to catch his killing stroke. She was on her feet with remarkable speed and aimed a kick at the off-balance fighter. Another grunt of

*surprise as she caught him in the midriff made her cackle with
excitement. The warrior had clearly not expected her to carry a
weapon, but he learned his lesson quickly, as he rolled adroitly
to miss the backhanded slash she aimed at his head.*

*She was between him and his sword now. She closed, baring
her dagger-like teeth and flexing her claws. She would make this
slow — he would suffer, just as Grendel had. She would hobble
him with a deft slash at the knee, like — She snarled in fury as
her cut was intercepted and the warrior grasped her knife-arm.
Before she could bring teeth and claws into play, she felt herself
seized in a bear hug, the breath whooshing from her. He had
spirit — this would be a fine kill!*

No one bore witness to the mighty struggle that took place in that
cave; the indestructible monster against the irresistible courage of
a hero. Up on the surface we waited for what seemed like hours. We
waited at first with expectation, then with hope. As the shadows drew
in and the daylight waned, our hope turned to fear. No one looked at
each other; instead, eyes were cast down and shoulders sagged. Scaife
lowered himself on the rope, but reported no sign of movement at
the entrance to the cave.

The Danes among our group lost heart, and they left us heavy-
hearted on the cliff top, the thirteen Geats and Unferth and I.
"I will never desert a man who carries that sword, for it has never
failed to find its mark," snarled the grizzled old warrior when the
Danes questioned why he stayed.

After more waiting, a sorry sight met our eyes. As we stared into
the darkening pool below, the water slowly began to change color,
dark swirls of rusty water appearing amid the fresh and clear.
Waegmund saw the stains in the water and turned to us with grief
in his eyes.
"That is blood," he said.

"Aye," replied Scaife, "but whose?" Without another word, One-Eye swung himself over the cliff's edge using the same rope that Beowulf had used. Sensing a purpose in my cunning comrade, I persuaded the Geats to tie up another rope and lowered myself over alongside Scaife. We hung there, hovering a few feet above the water, peering into the depths. After a few moments—a few moments that seemed an age of Man—Scaife shouted to me and pointed at the water. Amid the churning dark brown patches in the water, a series of bubbles was rising to the surface. The bubble activity increased, reaching a crescendo of froth and fury shortly before an arm shot out of the water clutching something that resembled a brown sack. Beowulf's body followed the hand, coughing and spluttering and shaking the sack at us. Scaife wrapped his legs around the thick rope and flipped upside down, holding his hands out to Beowulf. Beowulf, still fighting for breath, slung the brown sack in my direction and forced himself upward out of the water to cling to Scaife's outstretched hands. I caught the sack, looked up, and bellowed to the Geats on the cliff's edge.

"Pull!" I yelled, but my words were lost in the blustery winds above the churning pool. Fortunately, the Geats had seen everything, and strong hands grasped the ropes and hauled us to the top of the cliff. Beowulf lay gasping for breath and flapping his hand in my direction, while Scaife frantically rubbed some feeling back into his aching arms. Concerned, I seized Beowulf's hand. "Head!" he sputtered, in between spitting out mouthfuls of water onto the headland. I frowned, not understanding.

"Head," he sputtered indignantly, waving in the direction of the sack he had thrown to me. I picked up the sack, shouted, and dropped it again. Unferth picked it up and immediately began to laugh. He held it up for the others to see and shook it in my face, grinning. The "sack" was the head of Grendel, leering in a hideous death-grin, brown and wrinkled and covered in sparse hair like a . . . well, like a sack. The laughter broke the tension. Soon all the warriors were rolling around on the ground in merriment and relief, among them Beowulf, no longer sputtering—exhausted, but alive.

Beowulf's tale of the fight with Grendel's mother came later, back at Heorot, when food and warmth had brought color back into the hero's cheeks. The monster had been strong beyond anything Beowulf had experienced. He wrestled with her for an age, the cruel point of her dagger inching ever closer to his throat. There was nothing to brace himself against as he had done when tearing off Grendel's arm, and no weapon to ward off the blow he knew would come. Out of the corner of his eye he could see Unferth's obsidian blade lying on the floor behind the hag; somehow he had to reach it. His strength was failing, the strain on his muscles from the swim was telling, and he could feel the hag's breath in his face as she slowly forced his arm back and her dagger closer. They say in desperation men can do extraordinary things. Beowulf barely remembered how, but he had summoned one last burst of energy and hurled the monster away. She howled in anger and leaped back to attack, but the brief respite had given Beowulf time to throw himself across the floor and scoop up Unferth's blade. As the hag leaped on top of him, Beowulf reversed the sword—and prayed. He felt the beast's weight on his back, felt her hot breath on his neck and her gurgling cries of triumph. He gritted his teeth and waited for the final blow. But the gurgling had not been triumph; it had been the monster's death rattle as the sword pierced her seemingly invulnerable armor into her black heart. She lay still, blood seeping from the hole in her chest.

It took much of Beowulf's remaining strength to drag himself from under the monster's corpse, and more still to wrench free Unferth's sword. As he staggered back toward the cave entrance, he noticed another mound on the floor at the side of the vast, damp dwelling. It was the corpse of Grendel, cold, grisly, and stinking. Remembering his promise, the Geat brought Unferth's sword down and smote Grendel's head from his body—here at last was the trophy for Heorot. Beowulf took one last great lungful of air and clove the water below the cave, clutching the head in one hand. It was another hard swim, but his heart was lifted and it seemed only moments before he broke the surface of the water and sucked in the fresh air again.

There was no victory feast that night; we were too exhausted and the memory of the previous night's premature celebration was still fresh. Beowulf declared that the Geats would stay a full month to ensure that no further evils threatened the peace of Heorot. To while away the days, Hrothgar announced that games and sports would be held in Beowulf's honor. The hero himself declined to enter (to the relief of many of the warriors), and Scaife unsurprisingly proved himself a master with the sling and throwing dagger. I redeemed the honor of the house by beating the Geats in the horse race. Last, a great drinking contest was arranged between the Danes and the Geats, three from each band. Two hours later, five men snored loudly under the table while a triumphant Unferth chatted away as though he enjoyed nothing more than a sociable ale with friends.

At last the time came for the Geats to depart, and a feast was arranged unlike any the hall had ever seen. Heorot was awash with banners and decorations and tributes, and the cooks worked twice as hard as the last time to ensure that everything was roasted and baked and broiled on time. All the warriors scrubbed and polished their best tunics and armor, and the womenfolk sewed trim and lace onto their finest robes. The evening progressed much as the last feast had. The Danes took their seats and thundered their applause as Beowulf and his comrades entered the room. As they strode through the hall, Beowulf seized an embarrassed Unferth and raised his arm aloft so he could take his share of the applause. As Beowulf neared Hrothgar's seat, the old lord smiled and stood. The hall quieted.

wif

gif

hild

ādl

folc

þæt

tō

hord

mā

līca

Hafa

Gēa

fib

ɪnw

"On this occasion there is no need for me to leave my seat, Beowulf. You have your own." With a flourish Hrothgar removed a cloth from the seat next to his own to reveal a chair carved with elaborate scrollwork.

"This chair," proclaimed Hrothgar, "carries in its frame the tale of your struggle against Grendel and his foul mother. Each panel details part of that battle, so that long after we have gone, people can read the etchings and marvel at the deeds of the great Beowulf."

The Danes roared their approval, and roared once more when the doors opened and the queen entered with her ladies. Four of the ladies glided forward and laid down a parcel on the table in front of Beowulf. The queen drew back the ties on the parcel and opened the wraps. All eyes strained to see what it contained, and there was a gasp as Beowulf held up his gift. It was a coat of mail such as none had seen before. The coat was a series of fine links of hardened iron, with disks of beaten bronze laid over the resulting mesh. The mesh itself was sewn onto a soft leather tunic of great strength and suppleness. It was a gift without peer and beyond value. Beowulf thanked the queen courteously and sincerely. She bowed gracefully to him and to Lord Hrothgar and swept from the room.

When the commotion over the armor died down, Beowulf spoke quietly with Hrothgar, and the old lord nodded vigorously. The Geat turned to face the assembled Danes.

"Not all the heroes in these events were from among my people," he stated, looking coolly around the room. "Some among you put aside your fatigue and fear and joined us in our fight."

At this he turned to his comrades and they held out Unferth's mighty obsidian sword. "This blade was a gift from a Dane of outstanding courage," boomed Beowulf, holding aloft the deadly, featherlight sword.

"Unferth! Unferth!" shouted the Danes. Beowulf motioned them to be quiet.

"The sword belongs with your people, and I would return it to a Dane of outstanding courage."

"Unferth! Unferth!" The shouts came again, doubled in volume. Hands clapped Unferth on the back and urged him forward, but the old warrior stayed in his seat. Beowulf smiled at Unferth and nodded.

"Unferth is a hero, but he is a hero in his twilight years, and he would not thank me for putting on him any responsibility for protecting his people." Unferth nodded back his assent and drank down his beer with a scowl.

"But there is another among you who has shown his courage, leadership, and fortitude in these trying times." Beowulf paused dramatically and held out the sword toward—me! "I return this sword to Wiglaf."

I was aware of people pounding me on the back. I felt my face turn crimson with embarrassment as I was hoisted shoulder-high by the Danes and marched through the room past all my comrades and friends. I laughed at the absurdity of it all, but they banged their mugs on the table and chanted my name.

Set down in front of Hrothgar, I stood, feeling awkward and confused as he addressed me.

"Beowulf is right, Wiglaf. You have become a symbol of courage and loyalty to our people."

I didn't know where to look.

"And now," continued the lord, "Beowulf wants you to accompany him back to his home, so his people can meet his friend and comrade, Wiglaf."

I just stood there, stunned and stupid.

"What do you say, Wiglaf?" Hrothgar smiled, sensing my confusion. "Do you accept this invitation?"

"Er . . . well, er . . . yes, if my lord permits it," I stammered.

"Permit it?" boomed Hrothgar. "I insist you go, man. I will have these Geats know that we too have our men of wit and bravery."

The rest of the night passed in a haze, and the next day in a blur. I barely had time to say farewell to my friends before I found myself wading into the surf to board Beowulf's ship home.

* * * * *

It was five years before I returned home. The old king, Hygelac, was delighted at Beowulf's return, for his health was failing and he wanted to see his kinsman before he died. I saw two kings of the Geats die, for Hygelac's son fell in a sea battle against pirates from the ice-lands the following year. The old man had no more offspring, and the kingship could have been passed on to any of a number of cousins and nephews. But there was one obvious choice among these more distant kinsmen, and the advisers and councelors begged Beowulf to take the throne. Reluctantly he agreed, and there followed a period of peace and prosperity in the Geat lands. Beowulf was just and magnanimous to those who obeyed the law but fierce in punishing those who abused his tolerance. He earned the enmity of many petty lords who liked to take advantage of their positions of power, but he earned the praise and love of the shackled folk he freed from their tyranny. I joined him on many of his forays into the country to bring order and justice to the land. Unferth's sword became something of a good-luck totem for Beowulf's warriors and an object of fear for his enemies.

Leaving my new home was a wrench, but word came that Hrothgar was fading, and his son, Aeorling, had requested that I return and act as his adviser. The sword and I took to the water again, and I felt the same stir as I approached Heorot that I had felt all those years ago when I arrived as a youngster seeking work and shelter. Only this time I heard men whisper my name and saw them point as I strode up to the great doors and entered the hall. I marched up to Hrothgar's great carved chair and bowed formally. The old man was slumped, half asleep, but Aeorling—no youngster himself—came forward to embrace me admiringly. Gently Aeorling woke his father, and the old man's head rose from his chest. His eyes were rheumy, and he peered at me as if seeing through a fog.

"Who is this?" he asked. "Some new hero come to my hall?"

"It is Wiglaf, Father," said Aeorling, "come back to us from the land of the Geats."

"Ah, Wiglaf," said the old man, a warm smile crossing his face. "Good. Now the land is safe. It is time for me to go." And so he went, just like that. With his head on his chest he fell asleep, never to wake again.

CHAPTER SIX
A NEW PERIL

The thief moved carefully across the rocks by the side of the fjord. If he could find somewhere to hide among these seashore potholes and caves, he could evade his pursuers. On this stony ground they didn't have the advantage of their horses, and they were clumsier and less sure-footed. Spending all one's life peeping around corners and clambering across rooftops had its advantages! He leaped nimbly from rock to rock until he came across a small stream. The ground was boggy around the stream, and he looked for a suitable rock on the other side. There—he could just make it. He leaped with both feet, flailing with his arms for balance, and just about landed his feet on the far side of the stream. Unfortunately, the rock moved; it was only half-bedded in the soft ground and shifted a crucial inch or two when he landed. Arms windmilling, and biting his lip to stop himself from crying out, he fell into the marshy stream. It was quite shallow, but it was cold, very cold; furthermore, it was on a steep slope and moving quickly. He tried to grab for the bank but missed and was carried, slithering and sliding, on the scree of the streambed. Down he tumbled, lurching first one way and then the other, but never close enough to the bank to stop the downward momentum.

The light was dim but the thief could see that the bank ended just ahead—and he would be carried over the cliff! In desperation he tried to throw himself up and out of the water, but he succeeded only in turning himself over and immersing his face in the freezing stream. He surfaced just

in time to feel his feet slip over the edge. He moaned inwardly as he went over the edge to certain death, and then screamed with pain when he hit something moments later. Through a mist of tears, he looked down and realized that he had landed upon a gnarled tree stump jutting out from the cliff face.

As he waited for the throbbing pain to subside, he wondered why he couldn't have kept his legs together as he went over. But there was no time for self-pity; the stump was slowly falling into the sea, and his weight was accelerating that natural process. He looked around frantically and felt his heart leap. Just to his left and a little below was a ledge, and if his eyes weren't deceiving him, the blackness of the rock suggested it was the opening to a cave in the rock face. Maneuvering himself so he was hanging from the stump was a heart-stopping process, as every movement made it shift in its moorings. At last he was hanging by both arms, swinging gently to the left. A deep breath, eyes closed, and he jumped. Two heartbeats missed and he felt his feet touch the ledge; instinctively he put his arm forward for balance—and fell again. Not outward to the foaming rocks below, but inward, onto a damp stone floor.

It took the thief a few moments to adjust his eyes to the dim light. What he had assumed to be a cave he now saw was a dark passageway leading at a slight incline into the rock. There was a powerful smell coming from the passage, which normally would have deterred him from investigating, but the alternatives were limited, so he picked himself up and crept cautiously down the dark corridor. What little light the outside world had offered was gone, but the thief was used to prowling dark corridors, and he felt before him with his toes for hidden drops or gaps. There were none. The corridor grew darker and the smell grew stronger, and—yes, warmer, it was definitely getting warmer. It was a bit like being in a stable when the horses were cooped up during the snowy months. The corridor curved slightly, and as he rounded the curve, he became aware of a faint light ahead. The passage had sloped upward, but not enough to have taken him to the surface.

As he grew closer, he realized that the light was artificial, like a candle reflecting off of a polished surface. His heart beat faster as he realized there was a cave ahead. He almost forgot to feel with his toes, and only just kept himself from falling as he reached a ledge above the cave. The light he had seen was reflecting off of a polished bronze goblet. The goblet was at the edge of a large pile. The thief caught his breath as he looked down. The mound was made up of gold coins, jewels, weapons, and precious objects, all piled haphazardly atop one another, glittering and winking at him in invitation. What was less inviting was the huge sea-dragon curled around the foot of the mound, its chest moving noiselessly in sleep. The warmth was supplied by curls of steam from the dragon's flared nostrils. The thief felt his bowels turn to water at the sheer size of this terrible guardian.

The thief licked his lips, torn between greed and fear. He looked to his left and saw that the ledge wound all the way around the chamber and ended at another opening similar to the one from which he had emerged. At once he made his decision, thinking that surely one small trophy would be no risk to his safety. Holding a small spur of rock in the cave wall, the thief leaned out as far as he could into the cave. He stretched and groped beneath him, grinning to himself as he felt the handle of the bronze goblet. A quick swing of his body and he was back on the ledge, clutching at the wall while he regained his equilibrium and steadied his heartbeat. Within seconds he was away, up the tunnel opposite, which, as he guessed, led him to a concealed entrance on the surface. He chuckled to himself at his cleverness and put his mind to thinking how he could sell this priceless artifact. But he wasn't as clever as he thought. The dragon was old and subtle, and the balance of the mound was precarious and delicate. The removal of the goblet upset that balance, and other objects in the pile began to shift and disturb themselves. It would take days, but the mound would topple, the dragon would wake, and it would know instantly that something had been taken. Dragons were greedy, acquisitive creatures; they did not like being robbed.

Many years had passed since I returned to the Dane lands, though I received messages at intervals from the Geats, usually via traveling musicians or storytellers. One day, such a bard presented me with a scroll—it was unusual for Beowulf to relay his messages on parchment, so I read it immediately:

Friend Wiglaf,
We have shared many struggles and many journeys. I am about
to undertake another, and it may be my last. Two nights ago
one of my fief-holders brought in a thief named Egdabod. This
Egdabod had in his possession a goblet he had tried to sell to my
man. The goblet was old, and when the wise men saw it, they
knew it immediately. It was the cup of an ancient ruler who had
been slain in battle by a vengeful dragon. This dragon flies again;
ancient and vindictive in its malice and unrelenting in its search
for its lost treasure. It burns and kills not out of necessity, but
out of spite and to harm the race that harbors the thief. Tales have
been spreading of the devastation on the south coast of the
country, and the wreckage has been spreading farther inland.
As soon as the snows are past their worst, we shall ride to find
this dragon and kill it—or be killed.
Be safe, and think well of your friend and ally,
Beowulf

Be safe, indeed. I was forty-five and still strong, and I wasn't going to stay at home while my friend rode to his death. I went immediately to Aeorling and asked his leave to sail to Beowulf's aid, just as the Geat lord had come to ours many years before. Knowing the history of our bond, he nodded his assent, and I sailed within two days.

By the time I arrived at Beowulf's hall, the Geats were nearly ready to leave. There was a shout from among the men thronging the courtyard, and Waegmund, Beowulf's cousin, stepped forward to greet me and wring my hand in his giant fist. Beowulf himself was not far behind, clasping me to him in a bone-shaking embrace.

"All those of the party that fought Grendel are with us, those who remain alive at least," said Beowulf, a catch in his voice. "You complete us, Wiglaf." He smiled that familiar smile—only now creases appeared at the corners of his mouth—and said, "I knew you would come, old friend. Some things are meant to be."

"It is counted an honor in my land that I fought alongside the great Beowulf," I replied, "and I would not stain that honor by deserting you now."

A familiar one-eyed figure pushed quietly through the ranks. He patted my horse and whispered in its ear, not meeting my eye. Only as he moved away did he turn and look at me.

"Good to see you, too, Scaife," I told him, grinning.

The enigmatic warrior simply nodded and walked back to the hall. Beowulf chuckled. "Much in my life has changed over the years," he said, "But never Scaife. Didn't understand him thirty years ago. Still don't."

The warriors around us roared their approval of the joke, and we walked back to the hall, laughing and exchanging banter.

Thirty men set out the next day on the Dragon Quest. It wasn't a difficult trip—the peace Beowulf had brought to the land meant it was an easy place for travelers. As we neared the coast, signs of the dragon's ravages became apparent. Whole stretches of farmland were scorched to blackness; burned-out buildings and stunted trees stood stark on the landscape as if hit by lightning. Beowulf's mood became darker as the signs of depredation increased.

Eventually we found ourselves on the dunes of the southern coast of the Geat lands. Egdabod was looking around glumly and scratching his head. The thief had been made to join the expedition because he was the only man who knew the location of the secret hoard. Or thought he knew.

"You'd better not be lost," growled Beowulf, with a dark look at the thief.

"It all looks the same, m'lord," moaned the thief. "Scrub, bit o' sand, more scrub, occasional patch o' water."

Beowulf didn't have time to be angry. Before we'd even had a chance to find the dragon, it found us. There was a low rumbling sound first—I thought it was the fierce seas crashing against the rock, until I realized it didn't have the ebb and flow of water. The rumbling was punctuated with hisses and a kind of growling. The warriors looked around nervously; it was Scaife who shouted and pointed. Not a hundred yards from us a great gush of steamy air rose above the cliff top. Moments later a snout followed, and there were gasps of fear and awe as a long scaled body came after. Finally the tail— forked and lashing furiously in all directions—was whipped over the cliff's edge. The beast glowered at us as we stood, huddled together, swords drawn in a futile gesture of defiance. Until that moment, this was a band of men who laughed at fear. These were hard men, men who had seen death and slaughter and carnage and destruction. These men had stood toe-to-toe with the monster Grendel and with that creature's fearsome mother. But when this dragon raised its head and pierced them with its baleful eyes, they quailed, and when a blast of fire billowed from its mouth, they broke and ran.

Three remained. Beowulf nodded to his right, and Scaife slowly paced that way, both swords raised at the ready. I took my cue and moved away to the left, my shield in front of me, and Unferth's great-sword in my other hand.

We took a pace forward, the three of us, but it was only at Beowulf that the great sea-serpent stared. It knew where the real threat lay. Step by step we approached the dreadful monster; I could hear the hammering of my heart. It didn't comfort me, other than to reassure me that I was still alive.

When the dragon attacked, it was with unbelievable speed and dexterity for such a huge creature. It raised itself on its powerful back legs, spread its wings, and launched itself at Beowulf. As it moved forward, Scaife leaped nimbly around the wing for a blindside attack. Not only was the dragon huge and quick; it was smart. Anticipating Scaife's move, the dragon uncoiled its huge spiked tail and caught the warrior amidships. The force of the blow knocked Scaife clean off his feet, and I watched in horror as his head caught a sickening blow on a rock. Scaife lay still. I made a tentative move to the dragon's right; the creature gave me a dismissive glance and belched a ball of fire from its mouth. Just in time, I brought up my shield—it saved me but was now charred wood, and my left arm exploded with pain.

"Wiglaf," called Beowulf above the din of the dragon's roar, "behind me!"

As the dragon spat another fireball at me I rolled back toward Beowulf, coming to my feet behind his broad frame. The sea-beast brought its gaze back to the hero, a look of malevolent triumph in its eyes. Drawing in a deep breath through its nostrils, the dragon aimed a huge flaming blast at Beowulf. Beowulf put his shield in front of his face, with much the same result as I had, but his body remained unburned. The armor, gifted him by Hrothgar's queen all those years ago, had withstood its sternest test. Lowering the useless shield, Beowulf hurled his war-ax at the dragon's still-open mouth. Bellowing in pain and fury as the ax bit into the roof of its mouth, the dragon reared on its mighty hind legs as it prepared for a final lunge.

Shrugging the charred shield from his arm, Beowulf didn't wait for the dragon to attack but flung himself around its neck, dragging its head down to hack at it with his sword. The huge span of the sea-monster's teeth clamped on Beowulf's back and bit clean through the mail. Roaring in triumph, the beast threw back its head and reared again on its legs. This was my only chance. I sprinted forward, and with all my strength I plunged Unferth's unbreakable sword into the dragon's belly. It was all I could do not to get crushed to death as the serpent writhed in frenzied agony, tossing Beowulf to and fro in its mouth as it sought the source of the pain.

Chapter Seven
The End of an Age

The dragon's wound was deep and mortal, and the thrashing didn't last long. With a final groan and a puff of smoke, the sea-dragon crashed on its side, dead. As it fell, its mouth opened, and Beowulf was spilled out, his body broken and bleeding. I crawled—it was the best I could do—over to where Beowulf lay and took his hand. To my astonishment his eyes opened, and he turned his head a fraction and smiled weakly at me.

"It is over," he said.

"Yes," I assured him, "the beast is dead."

"Not the beast," choked Beowulf, coughing up bloody spittle as he spoke. "Me. I am done. It is over."

I started to protest, but he silenced me with a feeble wave of his hand. A shadow loomed over us. I looked up, frantically reaching for a weapon, before I realized that it was Scaife, blood pouring from a head wound, who stood looking down at his dying friend.

"Scaife?" asked Beowulf urgently. The warrior knelt to hear. "I would have you . . ."

"No," preempted Scaife, "not me, old friend. I have a mind to spend the rest of my days traveling. Let it be Wiglaf. He is trusted by our people and will lead them well."

I was confused. What were they saying? Beowulf fumbled at a chain around his neck. He beckoned me forward, and instinctively I leaned toward him. As I did so, he dropped the chain around my neck and slipped into peace.

When the rest of the troop found us, they hung their heads in shame to realize that their lord had died facing a beast they had dared not. One by one they acknowledged me, a foreigner, as their new lord. Beowulf's body was placed on a makeshift bier strung between two of the horses. His ax and sword were retrieved and taken along with us. As we traveled slowly back to the hall of the Geats, news went before us of the hero's demise, and in every village people lined the path to pay tribute to their fallen lord.

At the hall there were tears and sadness at the passing of so great a leader. I ordered the preparation of a great funeral feast, and the making of a formal bier on which to send Beowulf to his final rest. When the time came, six strong men carried the ornately carved bier. I led the way with Scaife, and we carried our friend down to his

warship in the harbor. The bier was placed on the boat, and the
torches prepared. After a few words—no great speeches, for
Beowulf was one for deeds, not words—the kindling on the deck
of the boat was lit, and it was allowed to slip from its moorings
on its final journey.

An hour later, I sat with Scaife by my side, watching the boat drift
out to sea, burning brightly, the flames having caught the sweet oils
drenching Beowulf's shroud.

"We shall never see the like again," I observed.

"We have no need," answered Scaife, enigmatic to the last. I looked
at him and raised my eyebrows.

"The dragon was the last of the beasts of legend," he continued.
"The time for warrior-heroes has passed. Man now need fear only
his own inhumanity."

Bīo

wur

þæt

cord

dōgo

ʹNi

gūd

ēnī

īce

fīſt

y m

pe ꞃ

ꞇge

THE END

Bīowulf maþelode —hē ofer benne fp

wunde wæl-blēate;   wiffe hē gear

þæt hē dæg-hwīla   gedrogen hæ

eorðan wynne;   ðā wæs eall fcea

dōgor-gerīmef,   dēad ungemete nē

'Nū ic funa mīnum   fyllan wo

gūð-gewædu,   þær mē gifede f

ænig yrfe-weard   æfter wur

līce gelenge.   Ic ðāf lēode hē

fīftig wintra;   næf fe folc-cyni

ymbe-fittendra   ænig ða

þe mec gūð-winum   grētan dorf

egefan deon.

Appendixes

f
rð—
yn
ſcol
ng! Ð
ʒeardu
fyr
ʒon aldo
ea, wuldr
f; Bēowulf

Bīo
gec
ne ā
ēofa
ān-
lgıa
am v
wıτ
mu:
anɪ
wıð
gār-
geoɪ
ēod
fo

Beowulf

Beowulf was the greatest of the heroes of northern Europe during the Dark Ages after the fall of the Roman Empire. The tales of his courage and honesty could fill ten books such as this. He was the greatest warrior and the finest king his people had known, so it is little surprise that the Geats fell on hard times after his death. He would have grieved at his legacy: when he killed the beasts that preyed on mankind, he did not realize that mankind without predators would become the most destructive monster of all.

Hrothgar and Hygelac

The King of the Geats and the Lord of the Danes were both great rulers. They each lived a long time—long enough to carve out their dominions in blood and fire and gold. Those were harsh times and hard days, and both overlords left many enemies among those they conquered and defeated. So it was that when Hrothgar and Hygelac and those few heroes who remained after them faded from memory, the dark times returned, and the rule of law once again left their lands.

Wiglaf

Sadly, Wiglaf's reign as King of the Geats could never compare with that of his predecessor. An honest and courageous follower, Wiglaf was never a great leader, and the Geats had scores of enemies just waiting for Beowulf's demise. Wiglaf did his best—he was incapable of anything less—but gradually the Geat territories shrunk in on themselves. By the time Wiglaf's grandson took the throne, he was little more than a tribal leader.

BIOGRAPHIES

Unferth

Unferth was not always a sour and bitter man. In his youth he was the finest warrior in Hrothgar's house. His own story of how his vanity and pride brought him low tells only half a tale. When Unferth was in his prime, he led a raiding party against a nest of bandits. In the battle he slew many of the bandits, and only as the bodies were laid out for a funeral pyre did he recognize one of those he had killed as his own brother. He was never the same man again, until he redeemed himself alongside Beowulf.

Scaife

Next to Beowulf, the greatest warrior among the Geats was Scaife the One-Eye. No one knew where he came from—he just appeared one day at Hygelac's court. Blessed with quick wits and unnatural speed, the loss of an eye to a slingshot barely lessened his abilities. Beowulf looked to Scaife for battle strategy and cunning—his answer was often no more than a nod, but the two knew each other so well that Beowulf could read volumes in the slightest of gestures from his companion. Not long after Beowulf's death, Scaife left his homeland to "see the world" and was never seen again in the northern lands.

The Sea-hags

Grendel's mother was old enough to remember the time when the two-legs were not so strong. There were many of her kind living in the dark caves by the rocky shores, and the boats that washed against the rocks and the solitary farms inland made easy pickings for her kind. Then came the men of steel and a time of hardship for the hag, her sisters, and their offspring. She was old, and not as strong as she had been, and her get, Grendel, had grown up weaker. The days of the sea-hags were over.

ƿÆT ƿE GAR-D

na in gear-dagum þēod-cyni

þrym gefrūnon, hū ða æþelingas el

fremedon.   Oft Scyld Scēfing sceaþ

þreatum, monegum mægþum meodo-se

oftēah; egsode Eorle, syððan ǣrest we

fēasceaft funden; hē þæs frōfre gel

ƿēox under wolcnum, weorð-myndum

oðþæt him ǣghwylc þāra ymb-sitten

ofer hron-rāde hȳran scolde, gom

gyldan: þæt wæs gōd cyning! Ðǣm eafera

æfter cenned geong in geardum, þone

sende folce tō frōfre;   fyren-ðearfe

geat, þæt hīe ǣr drugon aldor-lēase la

ƿīle; him þæs Līf-frēa, wuldres Wealde

ƿorold-āre forgeaf: Bēowulf wæs br

THE ARTIST

A NOTE FROM
JOHN HOWE

l
un
oā
ı pā
ndr
ɔmba
era wæ
one Go
earfe o
aſe lang
Wealdenɔ
waeſ brēm

The View from Heorot

Beowulf is a light in the darkness. Beowulf is the lost hero who cannot save himself from his destiny, although he ultimately wins every battle but the last—the battle no human wins.

How many other *Beowulf*s were never written? How many other *Beowulf*s fell into silence and obscurity when their telling dwindled? The stories lost ever outnumber those recalled, making the few that have come down through the haphazard gauntlet of time all the more precious.

My first experience of *Beowulf* was actually of Grendel, when I was in high school. At the local library, I was drawn across three aisles to the cover of the eponymous novel by John Gardner. A black-and-white rendering of the monster in a slithery crouch spread over the cover and across the spine—creepy and irresistible. I devoured the book in much the same fashion Grendel does his victims, speedily and messily (and with as little afterthought, I'm sure). Many years later I received a copy of *The Monsters and the Critics,* in which J. R. R. Tolkien stands up in stalwart defense of the many values of *Beowulf,* beyond that of historical artifact. I devoured this one much more slowly and thoughtfully, before finally reading a translation of the story itself.

I found the world of Beowulf to be one of texture and grain, where man's hand is visible in everything he fashions. Seen from a comfortable world made by machines, such universes hold special appeal. Without forge or chisels, the closest I can come to such craft is with pencils and brushes, the tools of myth-archaeology.

Beowulf is so much more than just a tale of monsters and flashing swords. Beowulf's refusal to surrender, first to the rending darkness that reaches into Heorot, and then to creaking old age where the dragon waits, makes for a beautiful and moving story. It may be a tale from the so-called Dark Ages, but would that our own age of enlightenment could provide flames as bright.

John Howe

rð
ᵻād
pāh,
ndra
ʒombaꞃ
eafera wæſ
, þone God
ꞃen-ðearfe on
aldor-lēaſe lange
wuldꞃeſ Wealdend,
Bēowulf wæſ bꞃēme

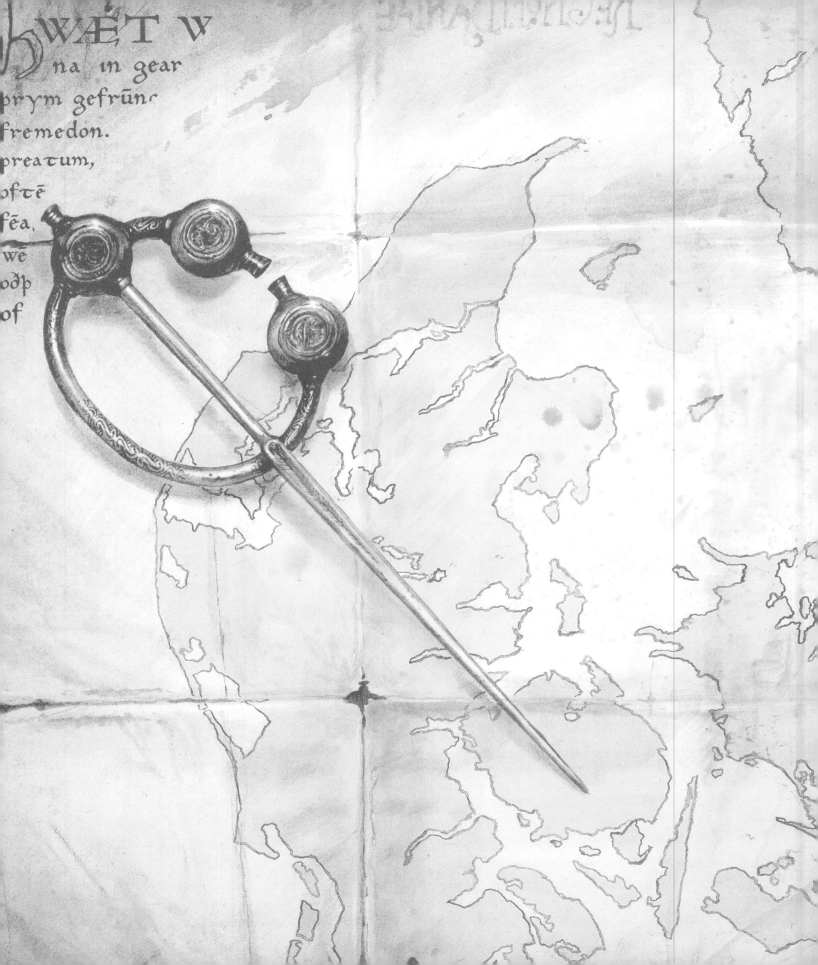

WÆT W
na in gear
þrym gefrūnc
fremedon.
þreatum,
oftē
fēa.
wē
oðþ
of